# VEGETABLES UNDERWEAR

JARED CHAPMAN

SCHOLASTIC INC.

FOR
JACKSON,
HUTCH
& KAMP

# UNDERWEAR!

# I WEAR UNDERWEAR!

# YOU WEAR UNDERWEAR!

# WE ALL WEAR UNDERWEAR!

DRAWERS!

UNDIES!

BRIEFS!

UNDERPANTS!

# THERE'S BIG UNDERWEAR

# AND LITTLE UNDERWEAR,

# DIRTY UNDERWEAR

# AND CLEAN UNDERWEAR,

# OLD UNDERWEAR

# AND NEW UNDERWEAR,

# SERIOUS UNDERWEAR

# AND FUNNY UNDERWEAR!

# THERE'S UNDERWEAR FOR MONDAY . . .

MONDAY

TUESDAY

WEDNESDAY

THURSDAY

**FRIDAY**

**SATURDAY**

**SUNDAY**

# . . . ALL THE WAY THROUGH SUNDAY!

# UNDERWEAR FOR BOYS

# AND UNDERWEAR FOR GIRLS.

**UNDERWEAR FOR BIG KIDS AND UNDERWEAR FOR BABIES.**

# WAIT A SECOND . . .

# BABIES DON'T WEAR UNDERWEAR. BABIES WEAR DIAPERS!

SORRY, BABIES.

# BUT THE BEST PART ABOUT UNDERWEAR IS . . .

. . . YOU CAN WEAR IT ANYWHERE!

# JUST REMEMBER TO PUT YOUR CLOTHES ON TOP.